Almost Starring Skinnybones

☆

Almost Starring
SKINNYBONES

☆ ☆ ☆ ☆ ☆

BARBARA PARK

ALFRED A. KNOPF ☆ NEW YORK

Copyright © 1988 by Barbara Park
Jacket illustration copyright © 1988 by Rob Sauber
All rights reserved under International and Pan-American
Copyright Conventions. Published in the United States by
Alfred A. Knopf, Inc., New York, and simultaneously in
Canada by Random House of Canada Limited, Toronto.
Distributed by Random House, Inc., New York.

Manufactured in the United States of America
6 8 0 9 7

Library of Congress Cataloging-in-Publication Data
Park, Barbara
Almost starring Skinnybones / by Barbara Park.
p. cm. Sequel to Skinnybones.
Summary: Irrepressible, twelve-year-old Alex is convinced
that he will be a star and impress his schoolmates when, as
the winner of a cat food essay contest, he is asked to make a
commercial for national television.
ISBN 0-394-89831-1 ISBN 0-394-99831-6 (lib. bdg.)
[1. Schools—Fiction. 2. Humorous stories.] I. Title.
PZ7.P2197A1 1988 [Fic]—dc19 87-28752

To all the fans of Skinnybones
who asked for a sequel . . .
You've got it!

Almost Starring Skinnybones

☆

☆ *1* ☆

*M*other Nature makes mistakes. I'm sorry to say that, but it's true. One of them sits behind me in English class. Her name is Annabelle Posey. I'd rather think that Annabelle was a mistake than believe Mother Nature made her on purpose.

Annabelle is probably the most stuck-up girl in the entire universe. Her father has his own local TV show. It's called *The Uncle Happy Show.* It's one of those little kiddie programs.

Mr. Posey is Uncle Happy. He wears a cowboy hat, a red rubber nose, and a cape. It's the type of costume you dig up on Halloween when you're too old for trick or treat, but you still want the candy.

Mostly all he does is show cartoons. Once in a while he has a guest appearance by this policeman called Uncle Officer. Uncle Officer talks about junk like bike safety and how you shouldn't yell out dirty stuff to cars when they honk at you or else the driver might come back and kill you. To put it nicely, it's not the kind of show that cleans up at the Emmy Awards.

But it doesn't matter to Annabelle. Even though no one in Hollywood has ever even heard of *The Uncle Happy Show*, she still brags about all the famous people she knows.

Like one time in second grade Annabelle actually stood up and told the class that God had come to her house for Sunday supper. I'm not kidding—God. The teacher practically called her a liar, but Annabelle wouldn't change her story. She said that he had wings, and a golden crown, and flew in her window and ate a chicken dinner.

Besides being a natural-born liar, Annabelle is also very good at making fun of people. Not everyone, exactly. Mostly just me. Like when she's asked to list her hobbies, Annabelle probably puts "reading, swimming, and making fun of Alex 'Skinnybones' Frankovitch."

Skinnybones. That's what she usually calls me. Her and about a million other kids at school. A skinny little bag of bones. Nice, huh?

I guess that's why I've got such a big mouth. Just

because I'm small doesn't mean I'm going to let jerks like Annabelle get the best of me. I get them before they get me. It sounds sort of dramatic, like a gunfight or something, but that's how it is.

This may seem crazy, but sometimes I think having people like Annabelle Posey around can actually be good for you. They give you a reason to keep trying to make something special out of yourself. To set goals and stuff. Then, when you finally make it, you can go right up to them in a real crowded room like the cafeteria and laugh in their ugly faces. My goal is to wipe out an entire lunch line with one giant "Ha!"

That's what was so great about my summer. I finally got my chance to make it big. Really big! And I owe it all to Kitty Fritters Cat Food Company.

Last year they sponsored a contest called the National Kitty Fritters Television Contest. You had to write an essay telling them why your cat ate Kitty Fritters. The winner got to go to New York over the summer and make a TV commercial!

I only entered as a joke. My essay was about how the fritters were real cheap and how they tasted like rubber, but who cared, because cats aren't people anyway. It was pretty insulting if you want to know the truth.

That's why I was so surprised when it won. I

guess the contest judge must have had a good sense of humor. In the letter the company sent, they said it was the most honest essay they had ever received.

Boy, did my father pick up on that one! For two solid weeks, he walked around saying how it should prove to me that honesty is always the best policy. He said it so much, I made the mistake of believing him. The last week of school I even decided to be honest with our substitute teacher. I went up to his desk and told him that some of us felt his feet were stinking up our room. They were, too. After he came in from playground duty, two kids in the front row keeled right over onto the floor.

He sent me to the office. I had to write a letter of apology.

Anyway, when I told Annabelle that I had won the contest and was going to make a national television commercial, she practically went crazy. She just couldn't stand the thought of someone else in town being a celebrity like her father.

"Big deal," she said, pretending to yawn in my face. "My father's made a million TV commercials."

I shook my head. "No, no, no, Annabelle. You don't seem to understand. This isn't a local commercial like your father does. This is a *national* commercial with a *major* pet food company. It's not the same thing as honking your nose, jumping off a chair, and shouting, "Watch *The Uncle Happy Show*!"

Annabelle stuck her snooty nose in the air. "So what? We're rich, aren't we? And besides, my father says that being a clown brings joy and laughter into the world."

"A clown?" I asked, astonished. "You're kidding. Is that what he's supposed to be? He's a clown?"

Annabelle looked annoyed. "Of course he's a clown, stupid." Then she paused a second and eyed me with suspicion. "Why? What else could he be?"

I shrugged my shoulders. "I don't know. I always thought he was just a lousy dresser."

Annabelle punched me in the stomach. Hard. I wasn't expecting it and let a loud *"Oomph!"* Then I doubled up into a little ball and fell over onto the basketball court. Walter Bingham strolled over and dribbled on my head.

When you're a skinny bag of bones, humiliating stuff like this happens all the time. It sounds funny. But when you're being dribbled on, you don't feel that much like laughing. Hardly at all, in fact.

Anyway, I was hoping a lot of that would change after I got to be a star. Being famous could really turn my life around. I dreamed about it all the time. Like about how I would get a fan club, and they would scream and faint and follow me around. And how I would make a personal appearance on *The Uncle Happy Show,* and Uncle Officer would salute me. And how God might drop by for a meatball sandwich.

One thing was certain. If I was ever going to become a big television star, I had to stop thinking of myself as Skinnybones and start concentrating on being a celebrity.

I began by signing autographs. Just to get the feel of it, I stood outside the market and wrote my name on people's grocery bags as they got into their cars. You wouldn't believe how excited some people got over a simple little autograph. One lady rolled her window up on my pen. Another guy started swatting me with his hat.

I just don't get it. Celebrity autographs are valuable. I've got a pretty good collection of my own. I keep them hidden in the bottom of my dresser drawer. I used to have them on my bulletin board, but every time my cousin Leon came over, he'd put his grubby little paws all over them; so now they're tucked away under my pajamas.

Mostly they're autographs of famous baseball and basketball players. Also there's one of Bugs Bunny. I was only three when I got it, so I didn't understand it was just some man dressed up in a rabbit suit. Personally I think it's the job of parents to keep small children from embarrassing themselves like I did. The guy actually signed my paper "BUGS."

Anyway, just because I signed some autographs didn't mean I thought I was as famous as Tom Cruise or anything. You don't get to be as famous as Tom Cruise by doing one little TV commercial. Cap'n Crunch or Mrs. Butterworth is about the best you can expect. Still, they're celebrities, aren't they?

The thought of me being a star really drove my mother crazy. I guess she figured it would make me stuck-up or something. Every time I talked about it, I got this giant lecture on how I wasn't a celebrity at all. How I was still "plain old Alex Frankovitch."

"I *know* I'm still plain old Alex Frankovitch," I snapped back one morning at breakfast. "But what's that got to do with anything? I can still be a star, can't I? I don't have to be a *giant* star like with a big mansion in Hollywood. I can just live here and be a *little* star with a little sports car and a little English butler."

My mother grunted and picked up the sports page.

"What d'you say, Mom?" I persisted. "A little sports car and a little butler? That's reasonable, isn't it?"

She didn't even bother to look up. "Of course it

is, Alex. Write down what you want. Your father and I will knock off a bank on the way home from work tonight."

My mother's a laugh a minute.

She wasn't the only one trying to ruin my fun, either. My father was just as bad. Like when we flew to New York City to make the commercial, he actually asked me to carry my own bag to the taxi. I couldn't believe it! What good was being a celebrity if you had to do stuff like that?

At first I started to laugh. "Are you kidding, Dad? This is a joke, right? You don't actually expect me, Alex Frankovitch—winner of the National Kitty Fritters Television Contest—to pick up his own duffel bag and lug it out to the cab, do you?"

My father totally ignored me. He just grabbed a bunch of his own stuff and started toward the big sliding glass doors. My mother did the same.

"Hey! Hold it!" I called after them. "This is nuts! Think about it! How many times have you seen Cap'n Crunch hauling his own luggage through an airport?"

My father stopped dead in his tracks and whirled around. My father's an excellent whirler. He can spin around so fast, it makes you fall down dizzy just watching. After he whirls comes the part I hate most. He heads toward me doing his Frankenstein

10

walk. Slowly. Very slowly. Real stiff in the legs. He doesn't smile either.

When he got to where I was standing, he glared at me a second and said, "Just out of curiosity, King Tut"—knowing very well that this wasn't my name—"exactly who do you think is going to carry your suitcase if you don't? Me? Your mother? The pilot of the plane? Who?"

Since I hadn't really given this question a lot of thought, I was forced to come up with something quick.

"Let's get a waiter over here," I said with authority.

My father wasn't amused. He pointed to a nearby bench. "Sit, mister," he ordered.

The way he said it made me feel like a dog. A dog named Mister.

"Listen, Alex," he began. "You wrote a funny essay, and your mother and I are very proud of you. You deserve to do this commercial. But that doesn't mean that you're suddenly a movie star. And it also doesn't mean that you get special treatment or get to order other people around."

Geez! What a place for a lecture. Right in the middle of the Kennedy International Airport! Filled with big ears from all over the world!

"Shhh, Dad. Could you try to tone it down a little

bit? The tourists from Guatemala are starting to stare."

"I don't care who's staring, Alex," he replied, even louder than before. "All I care about is that you heard what I just said."

"Heard?" I responded. "Of course I heard. The whole airport heard, Dad. People taking off in planes in Yugoslavia probably heard."

"Good," he said. "Then close your mouth, pick up your bag, and get your rear end out to the taxi."

Great! My rear end! Big ears from all over the world, and he starts talking about my rear end!

Angrily, I grabbed my suitcase and started pulling it across the terminal. As soon as my father's back was turned, I put the bag down and made a big face. I did the one where you stretch the sides of your mouth out with your thumbs and pull the bottoms of your eyes down. This may sound childish to a lot of people, but personally I still find making faces at my parents very satisfying.

By the time we arrived at the hotel, it was already dark. It was especially dark for me because during the taxi ride I had decided to put on my sunglasses. I don't care what anyone says, no self-respecting celebrity in New York City ever goes out in public without his shades. Not even at night.

My dad snatched the glasses off my head and

12

went inside the lobby. My mother just shook her head. I worry about my mother's head. She shakes it so much, one of these days it's going to get real loose, and she won't be able to hold it up anymore. It'll just roll around on her shoulders and become an embarrassment to the family.

☆

That night, after the lights were out, I slipped my sunglasses back on. I guess you could say I was still pretty irritated about the incident at the airport. After all, what's so wrong about wanting to act like a celebrity? Wasn't that half the fun of winning the contest? After a whole lifetime of being teased, was it really so awful to try to feel special for once? Didn't I deserve it?

I hardly even had to think about it. Yes! Sure I did! Of course I did! Alex Frankovitch deserved a break.

I raised my fists into the darkness. *Hear that, world?* I screamed silently. *Alex Frankovitch deserves a break!*

I rolled over and broke my sunglasses.

☆ *2* ☆

The next morning, after breakfast, we headed for the studio. I was planning to take a limousine, but as soon as we were out the hotel door, my parents started to walk.

"What? Are you crazy?" I yelled, hurrying along behind them. "Celebrities don't walk to work! They ride in limos! Come on, Mom. Dad? This is embarrassing! I bet the Fruit of the Loom guys don't have to trot to the studio behind *their* parents!"

The trouble with the streets of New York City is that even when you're yelling stuff at the top of your lungs, there's so much honking going on, your parents can't hear you. Also, there are so many people on the sidewalk, if you don't concentrate on where you're going, you could get swept away with the crowd and end up in New Jersey.

14

It was exciting and scary all at the same time. New York City reminds me a little bit of the zoo. A lot of the people look like they should be on the endangered species list. In just three blocks, I saw a girl with a ring through her nose, a lady pushing a poodle in a stroller, and a guy wearing a cardboard box.

When we finally arrived at the TV studio, we had to check in with a security guard before we could go up to the studio.

"Name?" he said to me.

I stood up as straight as I could. "Just tell them Alex Frankovitch is here," I announced, feeling very important.

He checked off my name and looked up. "What a thrill."

Once we were allowed to pass, we walked down a long marble hallway to the elevator. When the doors opened, a boy about my age strolled off. You could tell just by the way he walked that he was somebody special. Someone you should know.

As he passed, I studied his face.

"Hey!" I blurted suddenly. "I know who you are! The kid on that dessert commercial! The creamy dreamy pudding that melts in your mouth! Pudding Boy! Am I right? You're Pudding Boy!"

Slowly the boy turned around and pretended to shoot me with his finger. "You got it, Frederick," he replied coolly.

He blew away the smoke from his imaginary gun and put it back in his pocket. Then he spun back around and strolled away.

"Wow!" I exclaimed as the elevator doors closed. "Pudding Boy! Was that guy cool or what?"

"That guy was cool," mimicked my father.

My mother frowned. "He called you Frederick."

"Yeah, what a crazy guy!" I laughed. "What a kidder."

"That guy was cool," repeated Dad, who was starting to get on my nerves.

When we got off the elevator, we were greeted by two men. One was from the Kitty Fritters company. The other was the director of the commercial, Mr. Rose.

I hate to say this, but Mr. Rose was a major disappointment. He didn't look like a director at all. He didn't have on a French beret or sunglasses or anything. He was wearing a sweatshirt and running shoes. It's like he got out of bed and thought it was Saturday.

"Aha!" he exclaimed, pumping my arm up and down. "You must be Alexander!"

It sounded funny. Alexander's my real name, but no one ever calls me that. I was named after Alexander Graham Bell. The phone guy.

Parents do this sort of thing all the time. They

name you after someone great and hope you'll turn out great yourself. It doesn't usually work though. Usually you just end up as an ordinary person with a stupid name, like Abraham Lincoln Beerbaum . . . or in *my* case, Alexander Bell Frankovitch. After a name like that, even the nickname Skinnybones doesn't sound that bad.

Finally Mr. Rose released my hand. "Well, we're on a pretty tight schedule today, so we'd better get started. Mom and Dad can have a seat in the back of the studio, and I'll take our young actor friend with me."

Mr. Rose led me over to the set. A set is a fake place in the studio where the commercial is actually filmed. Sometimes it's a fake living room or school-room. In this case it was a fake kitchen.

Fake kitchens are very popular sets for pet food commercials. I'm not sure why though. We feed our cat outside. She only gets to eat inside if there's a hurricane. My mother says the cat food makes the kitchen smell like a stink hole.

Anyway, we weren't on the set for more than two minutes before Mr. Rose cupped his hands around his mouth and shouted, *"Makeup!"* Then, before I knew what was happening, this blond lady came bounding from out of nowhere, plunked me down in a kitchen chair, and started putting gook all over my face. It happened so quickly, it made my head spin. I didn't even have time to relax in my dressing room, or get a back rub, or sit in a Jacuzzi. And besides, even though I knew I'd have to wear makeup, I sure didn't want it to happen like this. Not in front of everybody.

"Er . . . uh, excuse me, Mr. Rose," I stammered as the blond lady turned me first in one direction and then the other. "Ah, I was just wondering if maybe I got a dressing room or something. That's what happens on *Lifestyles of the Rich and Famous*. They get a dressing room."

Mr. Rose furrowed his brows. That means he made his eyebrows look real annoyed. It's an expression that kids my age don't usually use, but I've had enough brows furrowed at me to know what it means. The main thing about furrowed brows is that they make me nervous. The longer Mr. Rose looked at me like that, the more I began squirming around in my chair. I finally got so self-conscious, I started laughing real stupidly—kind of like Goofy.

"Oh, *I* get it," said Mr. Rose, beginning to laugh along with me. "We've got ourselves a comedian here! Please don't scare me like that, Alexander. For a minute there I thought you might be one of those spoiled, demanding little child actors I usually get stuck with."

I was just about to ask if he meant Pudding Boy,

18

when he suddenly turned away from me. Then he cupped his hands around his mouth again and screamed, *"Bring in the cat!"*

The next thing I knew, I was sitting there with this disgusting, giant yellow creature on my lap.

Ronald. That was its name. Ronald the Cat. Without a doubt the stupidest cat name I've ever heard in my life. Naming your cat Ronald is like naming your kid Whiskers.

Also, just to give you an idea about how giant this cat was, when the trainer dumped it into my lap, I actually went *"Ooooff!"* I'm not kidding. I thought it was a kid in a cat suit.

The thing is, I don't even *like* cats. I mean I know I have one as a pet and everything. But my parents got Fluffy before I knew how to talk, so I never had a chance to tell them I hated her. I tried to make a few hand signals, but they didn't catch on. Every time a little kid makes hand signals, his parents think he has to go to the bathroom. I finally got so tired of being rushed away, I decided just to put up with the cat until I was older.

Mostly what I hate about cats is the way they're always sneaking up on you. I realize it's probably just the result of being born with fur on your feet, but I still think they could cough when they come into a room to let you know they're there.

Fluffy's the worst. Sometimes I'll be standing

around in the bathroom with nothing on, and all of a sudden I'll look down and there she is. And she's been staring at me the whole time and I didn't even know it. I've heard her laugh at me before, too. I don't tell that to many people, but I swear I've heard Fluffy laugh at me about five times.

Anyway, I could tell right away that the trainer and I didn't feel the same way about cats. As soon as the makeup lady left, he patted me on the shoulder and said, "Okay, Clyde, how about if you and Ronald introduce yourselves and get acquainted?"

I'm serious. This man actually expected me to say something like, "Hello, Ronald. How's it going, dude?"

"Uh . . . no offense," I replied. "But I'm twelve now. I don't really talk to cats that much."

The trainer looked irritated. "Listen, Sylvester, I don't care if you're ninety-seven. If Ronald doesn't feel comfortable with you, this could be a very long day for all of us."

I was about to tell the man that my name wasn't Clyde or Sylvester when all of a sudden I looked down and caught Ronald licking the front of my new shirt.

"Sick!" I exclaimed, pushing him off my lap as fast as I could. "Cat saliva! Sick!"

The trainer picked up Ronald and stomped off.

20

Behind me Mr. Rose made this little whimpering sound. I recognized it right away. It was the same sound my Little League coach used to make when I'd show up for a game.

Furrowing his brows for the second time in only minutes, Mr. Rose pulled up a chair beside me. Then he sat there breathing real slowly like he was trying to keep from losing his temper.

I felt insulted, if you want to know the truth. I mean, I know that directors have to put up with a lot of little brats, but I still don't think I should have been treated as one of them. After all, we're talking about a cat saliva problem here.

After he got his breathing under control, Mr. Rose put his hand on my shoulder. "Listen, my friend," he said, even though it was plain that I wasn't. "I understand that you're not a professional actor, but making commercials is like anything else. If you want to get something accomplished, the magic word is cooperation. Working with animals can be very tricky. And we've got to have cooperation among all of us—you and me and Ronald and Donald—if we want to make this go smoothly."

I almost started to laugh. "Ronald and Donald? Ronald's trainer is named Donald? Seriously? Ronnie and Donnie? Ron and Don? Ronno and—"

"Enough!" interrupted Mr. Rose. "Please, Alexander! Let's not make this worse than it already is. Let's just try very hard to cooperate with each other and see if we can't come out with a cute commercial by the end of the day. How 'bout it?"

"Er . . . cute?" I asked, suddenly getting an uncomfortable feeling in the pit of my stomach. "Uh, could you please explain 'cute' to me, Mr. Rose. Nobody sent me a script or anything. I mean, this isn't going to be one of those stupid commercials where a kid has to make a fool out of himself, is it? This commercial is very important to me, Mr. Rose. I've got to wipe out a whole lunch line with one giant 'Ha'!"

"A giant 'Ha'?" repeated the director, curiously.

I didn't have time to explain. "Please, Mr. Rose," I begged. "I just don't want to cha-cha with the cat or sing to the fritters, okay? They put people in the nut house for stuff like that, you know. This guy down the street from my cousin Leon started talking to his hair, and they had an ambulance come take him away."

Mr. Rose stared at me a second, then started to laugh again.

"Relax, Alexander," he said as he stood up. "I promise you won't have to cha-cha with Ronald, okay? You have my word on it. Now, if you'll just wait here a minute, I'm going to check the camera angles, and we'll be ready to start."

"Yeah, but wait!" I called after him, still feeling uneasy. "What about singing to the fritters? Or how about actually *talking* to the cat? I don't have to carry on a conversation with Ronald, do I? You know, like the kind where the cat nods his head up and down like he's really listening. I mean, I don't mind saying 'Here, boy,' or something like that, but I don't want to act like I value his opinion or anything.

"Hey, Mr. Rose!" I called again, even though by now he was hidden behind one of the huge cameras. "Did I remember to tell you that I'm twelve? Could we keep that in mind, please? Could we keep in mind that in some parts of the world boys my age are little generals in the army?"

From behind the camera came two hearty laughs. One from Mr. Rose, the other from the cameraman. Then I heard my father's familiar chuckle ring out from the back of the studio. I even thought I heard Donald laughing.

For some reason, all this laughing put me at ease. Laughter does that to me sometimes. It makes me think everything's going okay. Only this time it wasn't. This time I guess you could say the laugh was on me.

☆

It was the stupid kind of commercial. The kind I hate. Not as dumb as dancing with a cat, but almost.

They made me play the part of a kid about six. I swear. Mr. Rose kept saying the part was created for a kid any age, but it wasn't. How many twelve-year-olds run away from home pulling a little red wagon?

That's what I had to do. I had to pretend I was this little sniveling crybaby kid who was running away from home with his cat. I didn't have any lines to speak. I just had to come into the kitchen wearing a dorky hat and blow my nose like I had been crying. Then I had to struggle to lift a forty-pound bag of Kitty Fritters into a little red wagon. After that I had to pick up fat Ronald, wipe my nose on my sleeve again, and head out the door pulling the wagon.

Just as the door was closing behind me, this announcer's voice would come on and say,

"Kitty Fritters . . . because sometimes your cat's the only friend you have."

It made me want to gag, it really did. When Mr. Rose first showed me the hat, I felt so sick I had to go to the bathroom and splash water on my face. It was raccoon, the kind Davy Crockett used to wear. The kind with a tail.

But I had no choice, you know? Mr. Rose explained the situation very clearly to me. When I started to complain, he sat me down and said, "Look, kid, either you do the commercial the way the Kitty Fritters people want it, or you walk."

"Er . . . walk? Exactly what do you mean, 'walk'?" I asked.

Mr. Rose made his fingers walk across the table. "Walk," he repeated. "As in back to the hotel, back to wherever you came from. Walk."

"Ohhhh, *walk* walk," I said stupidly.

"So what's it going to be, Alexander? Are we on or are we off? Do you wear the hat and pull the little wagon, or don't you?"

I bent my head and tried to muffle my answer with my hand.

"I'llpullthestupidwagun."

"Excuse me, Alexander? I didn't understand you."

"I said, I'll pull the wagon," I repeated gloomily. "But I just want you and that cat food guy to know something. I'm going to be thirteen in a few months, and in some countries kids actually get *married* at thirteen. Like, take Borneo, I think it is. Somewhere in Borneo some thirteen-year-old kid and his wife are going to be highly insulted when they see this."

I paused for a second and put my face in my hands. "One person will like it, though," I mumbled, feeling sick to my stomach. "Annabelle Posey will just *love* seeing me humiliated like this. She'll be pointing and laughing for weeks."

Mr. Rose ignored me. I guess by then he had decided that ignoring was the best way to handle me. It's not though. The best way to handle me is to let me have my own way.

We worked on the commercial all day. I'm not sure how many times we filmed it before Mr. Rose was happy. He had an assistant who kept track. Each time we were about to film, the assistant would stand in front of the set with a chalkboard and say "Kitty Fritters commercial, take one" . . . or "Kitty Fritters commercial, take eighteen" . . . or "take twenty-four." I stopped listening after "take thirty-two."

Ronald was the problem. Ronald the Cat—the dumbest animal actor in the entire universe.

All he had to do was sit in the middle of the kitchen floor and watch me blow my nose and load the fritters. Then he had to let me pick him up. Think about it. How great an actor do you have to be to let someone pick you up? You could actually be dead and play that part.

Not Ronald though. Every time he'd see me

coming, he'd lie down and roll over on his back. Then he'd make his body so limp it was like trying to pick up cat-shaped Jell-O. To make matters worse, Donald kept running in, shouting, "Up, Ronald, up!" He waved his arms around like he was training an elephant or something.

Finally Mr. Rose got real annoyed about it. "Where the heck did you get this cat, Donald? The morgue?"

Donald took Ronald and stormed off again. This time when they came back, Ronald's face was wet. I guess Donald had been trying to revive him.

Anyway, after Ronald had cooperated once or twice and the filming was finally over, we went around shaking hands and lying about how well everything had gone. Then Mr. Rose gave me a pat on the back, and Ronald and I shook paws. The Kitty Fritters man said if I ever came to Cincinnati, he'd take me through the cat food plant and show me how the fritters were made.

Oh, boy.

☆ *3* ☆

After I got home from New York, I started getting nervous all over again. No matter how you looked at it, the commercial was stupid. So stupid, I was afraid it might backfire right in my face. Instead of being a big celebrity like I'd planned, I could end up as the school fool.

For the first time in my life I started biting my nails. By the end of the week my fingers looked like ten little bald guys. Every time I closed my eyes at night, Annabelle Posey would drift into my mind. I'd be standing there with my little wagon, and she'd take one look at me and her mean, high-pitched cackle would penetrate my brain. Then pretty soon other voices would join in, until a thousand different laughs were echoing all around in my head.

28

I'd cover my ears, but it never helped. The laughing was inside. And it was worse than any nightmare I've ever had.

My parents noticed the change in me. It must have been the way I kept pushing my vegetables around and around my plate at dinner. One time I molded my mashed potatoes into a coffin.

"You've got to stop brooding about this, Alex," counseled my mother as we sat down to supper one night. "You did a terrific job on that commercial. So what if it wasn't exactly *Rambo*? There's nothing wrong with playing the part of a wimp."

I looked up from my meat loaf. "Thank you, Mother," I said sarcastically. "That makes me feel a lot better."

"You know what she means," said Dad, trying to come to the rescue. "That's *acting*, Alex. Acting isn't who you are. It's playing the role of someone else. And the better you do it, the better actor you are.

"Besides," he continued. "I don't think the character you played was a wimp. He was just a little younger than you, that's all."

I frowned into my potatoes. "If he had been any younger, it'd have been a diaper commercial." The thought of it made me shudder.

My mother sat there for a moment, gazing thoughtfully into space.

"You know, your father may be right on this one,"

she offered at last. "When you think about it, the character wasn't a wimp at all. He was just a sweet young boy with a love for his cat."

I buried my face in my hands and groaned.

"A love so great," she rambled on, "that even when he ran away from home, he thought not of himself, oh no, but of his little kitten whom he knew he would have to care for on the road. And to show that great love he sacrificed his own nutritional needs by loading a giant-size bag of fritters on board for the kitty cat. And nothing, mind you, not one little crumb, for himself."

My father and I stared at her, hoping for a sign that she had been kidding. She hadn't been. It was scary.

But at least she was trying to make me feel better. And I have to admit, some of it helped a little bit. After all, there's nothing really *wrong* with playing a younger character. They do it in Hollywood all the time. And besides, it *was* sort of a nice story, about the kid loving his cat and everything. Not as nice as my mother made it sound maybe. But still, nothing to have nightmares over. Nothing to be ashamed of.

☆

Two months. That's how long it took before the commercial finally appeared on TV. I was sitting in the family room watching *Gilligan's Island* with my best friend, Brian Dunlop, when all of a sudden it just popped onto the screen. It really took me by surprise!

"Hey! Look! There I am! There I am!" I screamed at the top of my lungs. "Look, Brian! My commercial!

"Mom!" I called. "Come quick! My commercial!" I was jumping up and down. My heart was pounding a million times a minute.

I thought Brian would be excited too. Not as excited as I was maybe. Not hysterical, but at least mildly excited. Moderately excited. I mean, how many kids get to sit in the same room with a guy that's on the screen right in front of them?

Not Brian though. He didn't even jump up and give me a high five. He just sat and watched the commercial without saying a word.

After it was over, he took a deep breath. Then he turned slowly and looked up at me. You could tell he was fighting to keep a straight face.

"Nice," he said quietly. Then this sort of muffled pig noise escaped from his throat, and he exploded. He started rolling around on the floor in wild, uncontrolled laughter, until he was practically crying. Even when my mother ran into the room, he didn't stop.

As the two of us watched him circle the floor, a sick, nervous feeling creeped over my skin and settled inside me.

"You missed it," I informed Mom, suddenly joyless. "It's all over."

She thought I meant the commercial. I meant my life.

My mother left the room. I could tell by the look on her face that she felt bad for me. But she's not the type to yell at my friends and embarrass everyone. When someone's acting up, she likes to let me embarrass him myself.

I sat down on the couch and waited for Brian to finish rolling. I guess I shouldn't have been surprised by his behavior. This isn't the first time that Brian has been a disappointment to me. I've known him since first grade and in the past six years, Brian Dunlop has let me down a lot.

Sometimes I think he's the kind of friend that grownups call a "fair-weather friend." That means when everything's going smoothly, he's the best friend a guy could want. But as soon as something goes wrong, Brian sort of turns on you. Like if he and I are at a boring movie, and I start trying to hit people in the head with Raisinets, when the manager comes Brian practically jumps out of his seat and starts spelling my name out for the guy.

Anyway, even though Brian may not have loved

the commercial, he still shouldn't have started laughing at it. Not right in front of me like that. I finally had to slug him two times to get him to stop.

Besides, what was so darned funny? It's not like I hadn't told him about how I'd be playing the role of a younger kid. I'd even told him about the hat and the wagon. So what was the big deal?

"The big deal is that you fell flat on your face trying to pick up the cat food bag!" he roared. "My great-grandmother is stronger than that. You ought to come with us the next time we go to the nursing home. The two of you could arm-wrestle. We could get it on *Wide World of Sports*. Grandma Dunlop versus Alex."

"Oh yeah?" I argued. "Well, guess what, Brian. That's called *acting*. I was supposed to act weak like that. I was playing the part of a little kid, remember? And even though he was running away from home, he loved his cat enough to take the giant bag of Kitty Fritters with him. Not the bargain size, Brian. Not the economy size. The *giant* size. And he didn't take any food for himself, either. Only the fritters for the cat."

Brian stopped laughing and pretended to dab his eyes with his shirt sleeve. "Oh, I'm sorry, Alex. That's very touching. I think I feel a tear coming on."

"Shut up, Dunlop," I replied, clenching my teeth.

"And that cat!" he continued. "What a blimp! How far do you think you could get carrying a fat bag like that?"

This time I didn't say anything. I just sat there wondering if I should call his father at work and tell on him. It may sound crazy, but Brian Dunlop hates being yelled at by adults more than any kid I've ever known. Once when he was being hollered at by our third-grade teacher, he raised his hand and said she was giving him a heart attack.

"Come on, Alex," he said, finally catching his breath. "Don't look so serious. I'm only kidding. Can't you take a joke?"

"Sure I can, Brian. And if you ever manage to come up with one, call me and we'll celebrate, okay? Meanwhile, maybe you'd just better go."

"Go? Why? Why do I have to go?"

"Why? I'll tell you why. Because you're dripping with stupidity, and I don't want it getting all over my rug, that's why."

It was pretty clear that Brian wanted to laugh again, but this time he held it in and just smirked.

Now, I realize that there are probably a lot of kids who would have punched Brian for this. But as I said before, I'd already hit him twice, and with

Brian twice is my limit. After that, he creams me.

Besides, that's one good thing about being small. You learn to use your brain more than most people. And sometimes when you do, you come up with even better ways of handling things. I'd get the best of him yet.

"Listen, Brian," I said, suddenly calming down as I kicked the old brain into action. "Let's not get into a fight over this, okay? I mean, I'm finally beginning to understand what's happening here. I think I know why you're acting like this."

Brian rolled his eyes and gave me the cuckoo sign. He does this sort of thing a lot. It never stops me though. It takes more than a little cuckoo sign to stop the brain of Alex B. Frankovitch.

"See, Brian, way down deep inside you're probably going through a lot of conflicts about this commercial. On one hand you're probably really admiring me a lot, but on the other hand you might actually be a little jealous."

Brian continued with the cuckoo sign.

"And I can understand how these feelings could be confusing to you, Brian," I went on. "After all, one day I'm just plain old Alex Frankovitch, your best friend, and then suddenly, *poof!* There I am on TV! And you're wondering if I'll still like you when

I'm a big famous star and you're still an ordinary little nothing."

"Alex," he said, trying to interrupt. But I wouldn't let him.

"And I bet you're worried that I might not hang around with you at school anymore, and that I'm going to drop you like a hot potato and go with the more popular kids."

"Alex!" he shouted this time. "If you really want to know what I think, you'll shut up and listen!"

"Guess what?" I replied smugly. "I don't."

"So listen anyway!" he continued. "I think you're taking this whole acting thing too seriously. Even before you did the stupid commercial, it's all you talked about. About New York and Hollywood, and how you were going to be a big movie star and ride in a limousine, and how people all over the world were going to recognize you and—"

"I never said *all* over the world," I corrected, raising a finger in the air. "I said in most major countries and the parts of China with electricity."

Brian ignored me and kept right on talking.

"And then you bought those sunglasses and started signing autographs that nobody wanted. My mother said the last time she went to the grocery store, you ripped her bag."

"She resisted," I explained simply. "A fan should never resist. Someone could get hurt."

36

Brian looked at me strangely. "You said that Pudding Boy is a personal friend of yours."

I smiled and nodded. "Yeah. What a crazy guy."

"Listen to yourself, Alex!" he exclaimed. "Can't you hear how you sound?"

Before I could answer, he stood up and headed for the door.

I followed.

"Look, Brian," I said. "All I meant to say was that even though I'm probably going to be very famous now, it doesn't mean I'm going to change."

I paused. "Of course, I'll probably have to wear a disguise from time to time, but—"

Brian covered his ears and hurried out the door. Just as he was starting down the front steps, he stopped suddenly and whipped around.

"Oh yeah. There's one more thing, Alex," he said.

"What?"

He put his hand on my shoulder. "No offense. But deep down, I really don't admire you that much."

☆

After he was gone, I turned off the TV and sat down in my father's recliner. Then I gazed down at the ten little bald guys on my hands. I fought the urge to chew on their heads.

37

I pushed the chair back to the reclining position, stretched out comfortably, and tried to relax.

I closed my eyes.

Annabelle Posey drifted into my mind. She was laughing harder than ever.

☆ *4* ☆

The next day I stopped by Brian's house to get him before school. Even when we have a fight, Brian and I walk to school together. It's one of the unwritten rules of our friendship.

At least it used to be.

"Sorry, Alex. He's already gone," Mrs. Dunlop informed me when she answered the door. "He left a few minutes ago."

I was shocked.

"What do you mean, he left a few minutes ago, Mrs. Dunlop?" I questioned. "Why would he leave without me? He *never* leaves without me. It'd be like a crime or a sin or something!"

"Alex, he's—"

"I hate to walk alone, Mrs. Dunlop! Brian knows

it, too. I tried it in kindergarten a couple of times. A high school kid came by in a car and hit me with an egg."

"Alex—"

"Have you ever been hit with an egg at high speed, Mrs. D.? It feels like you've been shot. I saw the eggshell, but I just thought some of my bones had splintered or something."

Mrs. Dunlop stood there rolling her eyes. She does that a lot when I'm around.

"Look, Alex. I don't know why Brian left without you. All I know is that about five minutes ago, he yelled good-bye and hurried out of here. I thought you were with him."

"Well, I'm not. I'm here," I said, pointing to her porch. "And out there somewhere there's a high-school kid with a handful of hen fruit just waiting to catch me alone."

"Alex, I really think you're being a little paranoid about this. Kids walk to school every day without being bombarded with garbage from passing cars."

"You should have seen my shirt, Mrs. D. It was all slimy and sick looking. Worse than a runny nose."

Mrs. Dunlop winced.

"It was a new shirt, too," I remembered. "It said 'I'm a Little Dickens.' My grandmother brought it to me from the Bahamas."

Mrs. Dunlop made this big sighing noise and shook her head. "Have a nice day, Alex," she said. Then she shut the door in my face.

Mrs. Dunlop thinks she knows me well enough to treat me like that.

I figured that Brian was too far ahead for me to catch up, so I didn't bother to run. Besides, who wanted to catch him anyway? Walking alone wouldn't be as bad as walking with a traitor like Brian Dunlop.

Actually it didn't turn out bad at all. As long as you stay on the lookout and protect yourself, you're not in too much danger. Every time a car came by, I held up my history book as a shield. It may sound crazy, but wearing a double-yolker to school does that to a person.

After I had gone a block or two, I started to relax a little and think about the day I was going to have. I hoped it would be good. I'd spent most of the night praying that everything would go okay, that everyone would love my commercial. Brian says that God doesn't appreciate people praying for dumb little favors. But in my opinion that's what he's there for.

As I walked, I felt in my pocket for my autograph pen. I'd brought it along just in case, you know? After all, if anything could make me famous, it was being seen in the middle of a great show like

41

Gilligan's Island. I paused a second and smiled. Maybe there'd even be an unruly mob waiting for me at my locker.

"Hey!" shouted a voice, suddenly interrupting my thoughts. "Hey, look! It's him, Mommy! It's that boy!"

Wow, this was great! I wasn't even at school yet, and already I had been recognized!

I turned around. It was Ernest Wilson. Ernest Wilson is three years old. He lives at the end of my street. He can't remember my name.

"Hey, you!" he screamed again. "I saw you on the TB! My mom told me you're the Kitty Boy!"

Ernest was standing at his screen door waving his arms and jumping up and down. I smiled and waved back. I probably should have gone over and patted him on the head or something. But I didn't. It was getting late, and I wanted to have a little bit of time left for the unruly mob.

I stopped to put on my sunglasses. My fans would expect it.

A few minutes later I arrived at my locker. Disappointed, I looked around. No unruly mob.

The only person gathered at my locker was Ned "The Bully" Jankowski. Ned has the locker right next to mine. I met him on the first day of school this year. He had been trying to work his lock combination.

42

"Hi," I had said. "I'm Alex."

Ned had grabbed me by my shirt. "Listen, dude," he said. "Just in case you might be thinking about looking at my combination—don't. 'Cause if my locker's ever broken into, I'll know it was you, and I'll track you down until I find you, and then I'll put my fist right through your eye socket."

Thinking it over for a second, I nodded. "That sounds fair, Ned," I squeaked. "That would be good."

Since then I've tried to avoid Ned the Bully whenever possible. But on this particular morning I decided to make an exception. Who knows, maybe he'd seen my commercial. Maybe he'd like having a famous friend.

"Hi, Ned," I said, giving him a timid little pat on the back. "Er . . . did you happen to see the commercial I made on TV yesterday, bud?"

Ned whipped around so fast, his breeze practically knocked me over. "Let's get one thing straight, dude," he replied, grabbing a handful of my shirt. "You're a skinny little bone bag and I'm not your bud. Get it? And if you ever slap me on the back again, I'm going to reach into your skull and pull your feet out through your brains."

This time I actually started to whimper. I didn't mean to but a series of little whimpers just slipped out my lips.

"Ss . . . ss . . . sounds good, Ned. Right out my brain. A guy couldn't ask for a better deal than that."

Finally Ned released his grip and stormed away. I stayed at my locker and dusted off. Not a bad start for the day really. Any time I'm able to leave my locker with all my body parts, I feel lucky.

A few minutes later I headed for my first-period English class. As soon as I was inside, I hurried to put my books under my chair. Then I sat down quickly and pulled out my autograph pen. I took a deep breath and hoped for the best.

Annabelle Posey was already seated at her desk behind me.

I spun around and grinned. It wasn't a pleasant little grin either. It was one of those big, wide, annoying grins that makes you look like a jack-o'-lantern.

Annabelle Posey turned her head and pretended not to see me. I knew she would. Whenever I grin at her, she pretends not to notice. It was just the chance I was looking for. Before she could stop me, I took my pen and wrote my name on her notebook.

Alex "The Greatest Star of All Time" Frankovitch

"My autograph," I explained nicely when she finally turned back around.

Annabelle made this face like she was going to be sick. Then she ripped open her purse, spit on a Kleenex, and started trying to rub my name away.

I widened my grin. "Sorry. Waterproof."

Annabelle Posey's face got so red, I thought she was going to boil over in her seat.

"You big jerk! I didn't want your stupid autograph! Turn around! Just turn around!"

She screamed it so loud, our teacher, Mrs. Ballentine, stopped taking attendance and started glaring at me. Mrs. Ballentine has one of the deadliest glares in the business. There's a rumor going around that a few years ago she actually glared a hole in a kid's head.

"What's going on there?" she asked at last. "What's all that racket about?"

Annabelle held her notebook over her head. "He scribbled his stupid name all over my stuff!" she declared loudly. "He's ruined it!"

"Alex?" said Mrs. Ballentine, raising her eyebrows.

"I'm deeply insulted," I replied, trying to keep a straight face. "An autograph is not scribble."

Mrs. Ballentine seemed puzzled. "Why are you calling it an autograph?"

Ahhh. The moment I'd been waiting for. I stood up.

"Well, I wasn't going to mention it, Mrs. B. But since you brought it up, I might as well talk about it. The national television commercial that I made in New York last summer was shown for the first time yesterday."

Mrs. Ballentine frowned. It was the kind of frown teachers do when they think you're lying. "You made a national television commercial?" she asked doubtfully.

"It came on during *Gilligan's Island*," I informed her. "I swear. You were probably still here at school making up those test questions nobody can ever answer."

Her frown got deeper.

"Ask anyone!" I insisted. "I bet a lot of kids saw it."

I turned around and scanned the room. "How many in here saw it? How many saw my commercial?"

No one answered. Not one person.

I started to sweat.

"Oh, come on, you guys," I persisted. "You did too. *Think. Gilligan's Island*! The new Kitty Fritters commercial! I was the kid running away from home with the cat."

Suddenly, in the back of the room, a hand shot into the air.

"That was you?" blurted Raymond Vellenburg, astonished. His eyes were as wide as saucers. "You were the kid in the coonskin cap?"

"Yes! Yes! That was me!" I exclaimed. "That was me!"

"I saw it too!" said Cynthia Kendall excitedly. "I didn't know it was you, though, Alex. I didn't recognize you."

I felt so proud I almost burst. I stuck out my chest and nodded eagerly. "Yeah! It was me all right! Did I say that I made it in New York?"

Raymond continued to stare at me in disbelief. "Let me get this straight. You mean the kid who fell on the floor trying to lift the cat food bag into the wagon—that was you?"

I bobbed my head up and down some more. "Yup! He was me! I was him!"

Suddenly Raymond dropped his head and began slapping the top of his desk with his hand.

"That was the *stupidest* commercial I've ever seen! What a weakling! You looked about four!"

Giggles started across the room.

Beads of sweat popped out all over my forehead. Oh no. It was happening! My worst nightmare was coming true.

Why wouldn't they stop laughing?

"Oh yeah?" I blurted, trying not to show the

hurt. "Well, guess what, Raymond? That's called acting. Acting isn't who you are. It's playing the part of someone else. And I happened to be playing the part of a little kid. And even though he was running away from home, he loved his cat enough to take the giant bag of Kitty Fritters with him. Not the bargain size, Raymond. Not the economy size. The *giant* size. And he didn't take any food for himself, either. Only the fritters for the cat."

Geez, why did I have to say that? It was the same stupid stuff I had said to Brian!

Albert Ruppert, the class show-off, jumped up and pretended to play the violin.

Raymond Vellenburg collapsed on the floor in hysterics. "The *giant* size!" he roared. "Man, what a moron!"

A thousand different laughs started echoing around in my head.

Behind me, Annabelle Posey's mean, high-pitched cackle penetrated my brain.

I wanted to die.

☆ 5 ☆

It was the worst day of my life. The absolute worst. Even after school, things just kept going straight downhill. . . .

"Will someone please tell Ernest Wilson to go home?" I shouted when I walked in the door that afternoon. "He followed me home from the corner, and he's sitting on the step waiting for me to show him the giant yellow kitty!"

My mother didn't answer.

I got up and peeked out the window.

"Now he's in the new lounge chair. He's got his feet all over it!"

That ought to get her, I thought. Mention feet in a chair and my mother goes nuts.

I sat down at the table and waited for her to rush

outside and shoo Ernest away. I wondered if she'd use her broom and chase him around the yard.

"Come on, Mom!" I screeched when she still hadn't come. "Do something! Aren't you going to do something? He . . ."

I didn't bother to finish. Right in the middle of my yelling I spotted her note on the refrigerator:

Dear Alex,
    I got called in to work today. Should be home by four. Don't eat a lot of junk.

                                       Mom

Great! Just great! The absolute worst day of my life and no one home to talk to. A guy could explode, keeping a day like this all bottled up inside.

"It'd serve her right, too," I growled out loud. "It'd serve her right if she came home and found me exploded all over the kitchen."

A knock came at the back door. I opened it just wide enough for my lips.

"Go home, Ernest. I told you before, there is no giant yellow kitty."

"Yes, there is too a kitty," insisted Ernest, running to the door and trying to force his way in the crack. "I saw it on the TB."

I rolled my eyes. "It's not a TB, Ernest. It's TV.

And the giant yellow kitty was just for the commercial. I don't own it. It's not mine, okay?"

Ernest put his face and nose all over the glass, trying to see inside.

"You're making a disgusting mess on the window, Ernest," I told him. "Will you go home if I give you my autograph?"

I'm not sure he knew what an autograph was, but he nodded his head yes.

I grabbed a felt-tip marker. Then I went outside and wrote my name on Ernest's arm.

He went home happy.

But I still wasn't. Ever since English class all I had wanted to do was run home and try to get the sound of Annabelle's laughing out of my brain. And I wanted to talk everything over with my mother. And then she'd feel real sorry for me and pat me on the head and tell me I'd never have to go back to junior high again. And then I could quit school and get a job stabbing trash with a pointy stick in the city park.

"But *noooo*," I said out loud again. "Where is she when I need her? At stupid work, that's where! At stupid work, leaving me alone with no one to talk to. No one to pat me on the head. No one to call the city park and see if there are any trash-stabbing jobs available."

Well, okay. That wasn't quite true. There *was* someone home. It wasn't the someone I wanted, though. Not the someone I wanted at all. . . .

☆

She walked into the room and sat down beside me. I looked the other way and pretended not to notice.

She didn't give up though. I knew she wouldn't give up. She would just sit there like she always does, waiting, patiently waiting, until finally I'd give in and tell her my problems.

But not this time, I thought. *This time I refuse to talk. The last thing I need is for someone else to start laughing at me. I've had enough laughing to last me a lifetime.*

I pulled my knees up to my chest and buried my head. I'd pretend she wasn't there, that's what I'd do. I'd keep my problems hidden inside and not say a word. She couldn't sit there forever, could she? She'd have to get discouraged sometime.

I'm not sure how long I stayed balled up like that. All I know is that after a while I started to get stiff. Then I lost the feeling in my left foot. Was she still there, or wasn't she? I had to know.

I peeked out from between my knees.

She was still there all right. She caught me looking at her and winked.

"Oh, okay, Fluffy! You win! I'll tell you what happened. But I'm not kidding—if you start to laugh, I'm putting you outside, and I'm locking the doors, and I'm not going to let you in until morning! Do you understand, Fluffy? Morning!"

After that it just came pouring out. About how I thought this commercial was going to be the best thing that ever happened to me. Only now it was the worst. And how everyone had laughed at me in English class. And how in my other classes hardly anyone had even *seen* the commercial. And how Ernest Wilson had followed me home screaming, "It's the Kitty Boy! It's the Kitty Boy!"

Fluffy rubbed her head against my foot. I think she was trying to be sympathetic.

"You should have heard him, Fluff," I continued. "Hey, Kitty Boy! How come you ran away from home with that giant yellow kitty cat? How come you couldn't lift that big bag of food? Weren't you strong enough?"

That's when it started. At first I just thought she had a frog in her throat or something. But after a few seconds it was pretty clear that Fluffy was starting to chuckle. Oh sure, she tried to make it seem like she was purring. But her mouth was drawn up in this twisted little grin.

I didn't waste a second. Before she knew what

was happening, I picked her up and rushed her to the back door. Then I gave her the old heave-ho. After that I ran around and locked all the doors and windows.

This may seem crazy—locking the doors and windows—but that's how I felt. Everything was falling apart! And I didn't care how stupid I was acting. I'd act any stupid way I wanted to.

I was running around like a lunatic. Slamming things around and yelling. I wasn't talking to my hair yet. But almost.

When the front doorbell started ringing, I was still going strong.

"Give me a break, cat!" I screamed from the other side of the door. "You don't actually think that I'm going to fall for the old doorbell-ringing trick, do you? The one where you ring the bell with your tail, and I'm supposed to think it's a person and open the door, and then you run inside and hide?"

The bell rang again and again.

"Give it up, Fluffo!" I screeched. "You can ring the bell until your tail falls off, but the door stays locked!"

I heard a knock.

"Hey! I've got an idea! Why don't you try laughing your way in! You're good at laughing, aren't you, Fluffy?"

"Alex! I'm going to stand here about two more seconds, and then I'm going to come inside and kill you! Do you hear me? Now open this door, and open it *now*!"

Oh no. Something was very wrong.

A key was unlocking the door! I didn't even have time to take cover! My mother rushed inside and hit me on the head with the evening newspaper.

"Thanks. I needed that," I said, rubbing my head.

"Don't tell me," she exploded. "Let me guess! You thought I was the cat, right? There are places for people like you, Alex! Hospitals where you can putter around the grounds and not harm anyone."

"I was crazy. I'm better now."

Thinking that I might get another swat with the paper, I covered my head. My mother seems to think that hitting a kid on the head with a paper doesn't do much damage.

After a minute or two I decided it was safe to come out. Mom was still standing in the middle of the floor, glaring at me. She reminded me of Mrs. Ballentine. If the two of them got together, they could glare your hair on fire.

"Tell me something, Alex," she continued. "Just between you and me, do any *other* animals talk to you? Or is Fluffy the only one?"

I thought about giving her a funny answer, but I decided not to. She was waving the paper around like it was a bullwhip.

"Come on, Mom," I said, trying to calm her down. "I knew it was you. I was going to let you in."

"When, Alex?" she snapped. "When were you going to let me in? After my tail had fallen off?"

When she said that, I almost burst out laughing. Suddenly my whole day seemed funny to me. That happens sometimes. Things get so bad, something inside you snaps, and you start laughing.

"Oh, this is real funny, isn't it, Alex?" Mom asked. "I always think it's funny when I've had a bad day at the office, and I come home with a splitting headache, and I can't find my key, and I ring the bell. And then my son stands on the other side of the locked door and tells me to try and laugh my way in. I can't think of anything funnier than that, can you?"

I'm pretty sure I wasn't supposed to answer, but I was still feeling giggly so I gave it a try.

"I don't know. Did I ever tell you about the time that Brian Dunlop blew his nose on his sheet? That was pretty funny. See, he was having this dream that his nose was running and—"

My mother let out a loud shriek and stormed past me to the kitchen. I knew she wasn't finished yelling though. My mother's a marathon yeller. She

56

can yell for twenty-six hours and never even breathe hard. Even with a splitting headache.

"You're a real amusing guy, you know that, Alex?" she shouted from the other room as she banged the pots and pans around. "A regular comedian, in fact!"

"Thank you," I whispered so she couldn't hear. "Thank you very much." Then I bowed.

"As a matter of fact," she continued, "you're so funny, why don't you march right up to your room and laugh at yourself until dinner?"

I waited to see if she was serious.

"Did you hear me, Alex? March!"

My mother's very big on marching. It makes her feel like a marine.

I headed for my room. I didn't march though. And once I got there, I didn't laugh anymore either. I don't know why. I guess I'd just used it all up.

I sat down on my bed and put my face in my pillow. After a second or two my eyes started watering a little. Not bad enough to need a Kleenex, but enough to know the wet was there.

I sat up and looked in the mirror. My nose was getting red. My hair was sticking out all over my head.

"Some star," I said out loud. "Some great star."

Then I buried my face in my pillow again.

☆ 6 ☆

Real life is almost never like the movies. In the movies if something bad happens to a kid, something good happens to make it all better. Like if a kid is accidentally run over by a steamroller, he'll end up winning the Olympics and get his picture on a Wheaties box.

Stuff like that doesn't happen in real life though. In real life if you're accidentally run over by a steamroller you just sit around the hospital all flat. You practically never end up on cereal.

You never get to drop out of school and work in the park either. Even after I finally told my parents about the rotten things that had happened to me, they still made me go back to school the next day.

I didn't stop trying though. That's the great thing about me. I hardly ever give up.

58

"Put the pointy stick away, Alex," ordered my father one night as we were watching TV. "For the last time, you're not dropping out of junior high. Your school years are the best years of your life."

I speared a gum wrapper lying next to the table. "I could be good at this. I know I could."

My mother sighed and shook her head. "I told you before, Alex. You expected too much. Friends will disappoint you sometimes. It happens to all of us."

"They're not my friends," I informed her for the millionth time. "Alex Frankovitch has no friends."

"Brian's still your friend," she offered. "At least the two of you are walking to school together again."

I frowned. "Big deal. He said I was a habit."

"Well, what about everyone who has called to say how much they *liked* the commercial, Alex? What do you call them?"

"I call them Nanna and Pop Pop," I replied, rolling my eyes.

My mother just shook her head. I swear, it's getting looser by the minute.

Just then a familiar little tune filled the room. I didn't have to look up to know what it was. It was the Kitty Fritters jingle. My commercial was on TV again.

Like so many other times that week, I tried my best not to watch. I hid my head in the chair cushion and covered up with my arms. I pretended to be ashamed. It was no use though. After only a second or two, I found myself peeking at the screen. The truth is, even after all I'd been through, I was still a big fan of mine.

Seeing myself on television continued to amaze me. Every time it happened, my eyes opened wide and my heart began to pound. I even started to smile a little. I couldn't help it. I just did.

It's too bad, you know. Too bad that there are mean people in the world who try to make you feel ashamed when you should feel proud. Seeing yourself on national television shouldn't make you hide your head in the chair cushion. It just shouldn't.

☆

We had an assembly at school the next day. I missed English class. On my way to the auditorium I stuck my head in the principal's office and shouted, "Thank you!" No one needed a school assembly more than I did. Even if it was stupid—even if it was the history teacher giving another boring slide show of his trip to Peru—no one wanted a break from school more than me.

When Brian and I walked into the auditorium that morning, Mrs. Wallin, the principal, was already at the microphone. She was shouting for everyone to be quiet.

60

"Students, please!" she begged. "As soon as you quiet down, we can get started!"

I don't know why principals waste their time saying stuff like that. It takes forever if you ask politely. If I were a principal, I'd just take out a gun and shoot someone in the foot.

As things started to settle down I noticed that Annabelle Posey was sitting right in front of me. For days she had done nothing but make fun of me. She'd sit behind me in English and hum the "Ballad of Davy Crockett" in my ear or call me Alex Frankfritters.

"Oh my gosh, Brian!" I gasped when I saw her stupid head in front of me. "Look! Up in the sky! It's a bird . . . it's a plane . . . it's Super . . . no, wait! I'm wrong! It's not Superman at all, Brian. Hold everything! It's coming closer into view . . .

"I can see it better now. There's a cape . . . yes, there's a cape all right. But wait! There's a cowboy hat . . . and, oh no, a big rubber nose!"

"Oh wow, Alex!" Brian gasped. "You don't mean it's . . ."

"Yes, Brian. I'm afraid I do. It's Uncle Dippy. Uncle Dippy, the flying cowboy clown. Flying his way into hundreds of homes each day, trying to find someone who can figure out what he is."

Without even turning around in her chair, Annabelle began sniffing the air.

61

"Does anyone here smell something?" she asked loudly. Sniff, sniff. . . .

"Like maybe someone's wearing a raccoon on their head."

A lot of kids seemed to think this was real funny. Brian was one of them. He made that pig sound again.

Just then Mrs. Wallin started clapping her hands to get our attention.

"And now, boys and girls," she announced. "Without wasting any more time, I'd like to introduce you all to our guest this morning. He's a fabulous magician and I know that many of you have heard of him. We're delighted to have him with us. So please give a big round of applause to . . . the Amazing Mel!"

The curtain opened and this man jumped out from behind a screen. He was wearing a top hat and a black tuxedo with big silver lapels that sparkled under the lights. Also, he had a rabbit sitting on his head. You couldn't see it, but when he bowed, he took off the hat and pulled the rabbit out, so you knew it had been sitting on his head for a while.

"Thank you. Thank you. Thank you," he gushed.

"Geez! What kind of magician is this guy, anyway?" I asked. "What kind of dumb name is the Amazing Mel?"

"Shh!" whispered Brian, concentrating very hard on the stage. Brian is one of those kids who thinks magic is really magic.

On stage Amazing Mel got right down to business. He grabbed a handful of skinny balloons and started blowing them up and twisting them into funny animal shapes.

He wasn't very good at it. Even when he told you what they were, you couldn't recognize them. The cat looked deformed. Like, instead of growing four legs, it grew three legs and a thumb.

"Okay. How many of you buckaroos recognize this little fella?" he said, holding one of his creations in the air.

"A mutant creature from the planet Zircon!" shouted someone from the back of the room. A second later he was led out of the auditorium by Mr. Armanti, the assistant principal.

"Thank you! Thank you! Thank you!" exclaimed Mel as he came to the end of the balloon act. Then he bowed and bowed until we started clapping again.

Mel tapped on his magic wand and turned it into a bunch of paper flowers.

"Thank you. Thank you. Thank you," he repeated.

"You're welcome. You're welcome. You're welcome," I replied, rolling my eyes.

It became pretty clear that the Amazing Mel was different from the magicians I've seen on TV. He didn't tell jokes or kid around with the audience like most of them do. He'd just perform a couple of easy tricks, say, "Thank you, thank you, thank you," and then go on to something else.

The tricks were the same old ones you've seen a million times before: card tricks, rope tricks, that kind of thing. Nothing spectacular. He made some milk disappear in his hat, but it wasn't anything a sponge couldn't do.

In some ways it really started to annoy me. All I kept thinking about was how the Amazing Mel was up on stage acting like a big star, and I was sitting in the audience being my usual nothing. It wasn't fair. Kids were applauding him like he was David Copperfield or something, and the guy had never even been on national television!

Finally, after about fifteen minutes, the Amazing Mel walked to the microphone. Then he wiped his forehead like these stupid tricks were taking a lot of effort or something.

"Thank you. Thank you. Thank you," he said breathlessly. "Now then, for my next few tricks I have a little surprise for you. I'm going to need an assistant! How about it buckaroos! Is there anyone out there who'd like to come join me on stage?"

Wait a minute! Join him on stage? Is *that* what he had said? Had he asked for a volunteer?

I didn't even have to think about it. Me! It had to be me! It would be perfect! I could stand on the stage and say my name and everyone in the whole school would see me. Maybe a few kids would even recognize me! That'd show Annabelle Posey and her stupid friends. They'd even have to clap for me. How could they clap for Mel and not clap for me at the same time?

I shot my hand in the air and began waving it around like crazy.

"Ooooh! Ooooh!" I said, straining to raise it higher and higher. But the Amazing Mel didn't see me. Too many other hands were blocking me out. "Yo, Mel! Right here!" I screamed out. "Yo, Mel!"

Brian looked at me with disapproval. "Yo, Mel?" he repeated. "You're shouting, 'Yo, Mel,' to a famous magician?"

I couldn't waste another second. Mel was getting ready to pick. He had his finger all pointed and ready to go!

Quickly I sprang from my seat and headed for the main aisle.

"Oh no, Alex! Come on!" called Brian, grabbing for my shirt. "You were just getting back to normal!"

I heard him, but I didn't stop. When I got to the

main aisle, I blitzed for the stage. I'm not kidding. It was just like on *The Price Is Right*.

I could hear a few kids starting to laugh, but I didn't care. All I cared about was getting on the stage, where I belonged.

Out of breath, I zoomed up the steps and ran toward the magician. When he saw me flying in his direction, the Amazing Mel got a funny look on his face. Scared, sort of. Like I had just zoomed in from a mental hospital or something.

"Er . . . ah, who do we have here?" he asked hesitantly.

I held out my hand. But before I could answer, someone from the audience answered for me.

"Oh no! Look! It's Skinnybones! Oh, man! Not Skinnybones!"

And at that moment it seemed like the whole world started laughing at me at once. Skinnybones! God! How I hate to be called that stupid name! Why did they have to call me that?

For a second I tried laughing along with them. You know, trying to make it seem like I didn't mind being ridiculed. But inside I was dying. This wasn't the way I had it planned. Why couldn't things ever be the way I had them planned?

My face was turning red. I could feel it.

The Amazing Mel looked confused. "Er, what was the name again?"

66

He held out the microphone for me to answer.

"Uh, Harold," I blurted. "Harold Hiney."

The place exploded in laughter. I did too. I don't know where it came from. Harold Hiney. It just popped into my head and I said it.

The Amazing Mel didn't think I was funny at all. He rushed me away from the microphone and hurried to begin the next trick. First he stood me out of the way. Then he held his magic hat up to the audience to show it was empty. I tried to lean forward and see inside, but he wouldn't let me.

"Ugga-bugga-boop-boop!" he said, as if seventh graders actually believe in stupid magic words. Then he waved his wand across the top of the hat.

A second later the Amazing Mel started pulling beautiful colored silk scarves from the hat and giving them to me to hold.

A few kids were still laughing, but most of them were concentrating on the trick. Meanwhile Mel kept pulling more and more scarves out of the hat and giving them to me.

The bright purple one was the prettiest, I thought. When he handed it to me, I held it up for everyone to see. First one side, then the other, just the way a good assistant should.

Then I blew my nose in it.

I don't mean I *really* blew my nose in it. I just pretended to. Just to be funny, you know? I held the

67

purple scarf up to my face and did this big nose-blow sound with my mouth. It sounded real, too.

The audience started roaring all over again. It was kind of a thrill, if you want to know the truth. Sort of like I was in control of things. Like I could make them laugh any time I wanted to.

Mel hadn't seen what I had done with the purple scarf, but he definitely heard the nose blow. When he turned around, he had this real grouchy look on his face.

"Heh heh," I giggled sheepishly. "Heh heh heh."

Irritated, the Amazing Mel handed me the top hat and snarled something at me. I think it was something about putting the scarves away. Then he turned back around to get ready for his next trick.

I stood there staring at the hat in my hands. I don't know why, but I've always wanted to try on a top hat. I guess it's because a top hat makes you look distinguished. Even a dirty old bum looks distinguished in a top hat. Even if he's eating out of a pork-and-bean can.

The hat looked too big, but I decided to give it a try anyway. After all, a kid doesn't really get that many chances to look distinguished. I got to be Old King Cole in a school program once, but I don't think I looked that dignified. Old King Cole was a merry old soul. That means he was a simpleton.

I was right about the hat being big. As soon as I put it on my head, it fell over my nose and ears, right down to my chin.

I could hear the audience start to crack up, but I didn't take it off. I just stood there quietly in the dark, rocking back and forth on my heels. Just minding my own business. After a second I took a step toward the microphone and started to whistle a little tune in there.

Since I couldn't see, I'm not exactly sure what happened next. All I know is that after a second or two I felt the hat being lifted from my head and the Amazing Mel was staring down at me. He was sneering. Something told me I was finished being his assistant.

He shook my hand and led me over to the stage steps. I'm pretty sure he never "thanked me, thanked me, thanked me." At least I didn't hear him. Just as I was about to leave the stage, everyone in the auditorium started applauding so loud, you couldn't hear anything else.

I looked out over the crowd. That's when it hit me. It was for me! All that applause—it was just for me! Me! Alexander Bell Frankovitch!

I couldn't believe it. It was like a dream come true. If you've ever been applauded, you know what I'm talking about.

Even when my parents tell me they love me, it's not as good as applause. Let's face it, my parents *have* to love me. It's like a law or something. But nobody has to clap. Not unless they want to. Nope, nobody *ever* has to clap.

The tippy top. That's what I used to call it when I was three. Whenever my parents would take me to get an ice cream sundae, I'd start jumping up and down at the counter screaming, "And put a cherry right on the tippy top!"

That's where I was after the magic show. Right on the tippy top. So high up, I could feel people looking up to me as I walked down the hall. Kids I'd never even seen before pointed at me as I went back to class. "Hey! That's him!" I heard them whisper. "The kid from the magic show!"

At lunch Chad Jones gave me free cuts in line. I've been eating lunch at school for seven years and this was the first time I ever got free cuts. Last year I tried shoving my way in front of a first grader, and the girls' gym teacher picked me up and carried me back to the end.

Anyway, I was standing there giving old Chad a few pointers on his fake nose blow when Annabelle Posey and two of her snobby friends walked into the cafeteria and lined up near the door.

I didn't even hesitate. Not for a second. I jumped out of line so quick, it made Chad's head spin. Then I took a deep breath and waited. Waited for Annabelle Posey to look up.

"Ha!" I bellowed the instant she saw me.

Annabelle jumped! It had been the best "Ha!" of my career. It had erupted from deep inside me, from the place where frustrations stay all bottled up until you can't stand them anymore. It sounded mean and mocking at the same time. It echoed off the cafeteria walls.

Annabelle rolled her eyes in disgust and pointed. "You were so stupid in that assembly, I couldn't believe it! You made a total fool of yourself!"

Loudly, I clapped my hands together to get everyone's attention. "Excuse me!" I yelled above the cafeteria noise. "But did anyone happen to see the end of *The Uncle Happy Show* this morning? I missed it, and it's driving me crazy. I turned it off just as Uncle Happy was about to squirt Mr. Billy-Bob with his seltzer bottle."

Anyone who heard me started to laugh. Annabelle's face turned a hundred shades of red. After a second or two she ran out of the room.

I stepped back in line and gave Chad a high five. I bought myself an extra package of Twinkies to celebrate.

The two of us paid for our lunches and headed for the table. It was already pretty full. But when Willy Mumford and Raymond Vellenburg saw me coming, they squished together and made a place for me. I couldn't believe it! Usually I have to force my way in, turn my tray around, and eat my lunch sideways.

All anyone talked about was the assembly. "You should have seen the sick expression on Mel's face when you blew your honker in his scarf!" roared Willy. "I thought he was going to barf up that pigeon he pretended to swallow!"

Suddenly a boy sitting at the table behind me started tapping me on the back. "That was you! Right? You're the kid from the show!"

I waited a second before I slowly turned around to face him. Then I gave him this real casual nod and pretended to shoot him with my finger. "You got it, Frederick," I replied cooler than anything.

I blew the imaginary smoke away.

I'm serious. I was cooler than cool.

☆

That night at dinner, I couldn't sit still. You don't have to act cool with your parents. They don't understand it anyway.

"You should have been there!" I exclaimed. "The whole place was cracking up. I swear! I had that audience right in the palm of my hand! They loved me!"

My father gave a reluctant smile. Mom patted my arm. I guess I should have known they wouldn't jump up and down or anything. They only get excited about unimportant stuff. Like if the cap is off the toothpaste.

"We're glad you had a good day, Alex," replied my mother, hardly sounding glad at all. "Just don't count on anything to change, okay? I'd hate to see you disappointed again. You know how you felt when they didn't like your commercial."

"But don't you see? That's the great thing about this!" I explained. "There's nothing to count on, it's already happened! I'm already a hit! There's even been talk of a fan club!"

The two of them looked at each other and quickly left the kitchen. I think they went somewhere to roll their eyes and groan.

I wasn't kidding though. By Saturday my fan club had four members. I wanted to keep it small. Just close personal friends and relatives. Even though

Brian hadn't joined yet, I offered him the chance to be president. He stared at me a second and pushed me down.

"I'm serious!" I called as he walked away. "Think about it! This could be a chance of a lifetime. You could finally be in charge of something. You could call meetings and shout, 'Come to order!' I bet we could even get you one of those little wooden mallets."

Suddenly he spun around and headed back in my direction. He continued coming until his mouth was about an inch from my ear.

"No!" he screamed as loud as he could. "Did you hear me, Alex, you giant jerk? No! No! No! No! No!"

Without waiting for me to respond, he turned and stormed away again.

I just shook my head and smiled. What a kidder.

"Let's do lunch, you crazy guy," I called after him.

☆

The first meeting was held at my house on Saturday morning. Nanna and Pop Pop couldn't make it. They wanted to. But they live in Florida.

The other two members showed up. But with only the three of us it was a little bit of a letdown.

Fluffy refused to wear her nametag, and Ernest Wilson wet his pants and had to run home.

Luckily, at school things just kept getting better and better. Even though most of the guys had stopped talking about the magic show, they still saved a place for me at the lunch table. Why wouldn't they? I was the best thing that had happened to that table since Butch Botts made milk come out his nose.

On Tuesday Tyrone Hayes asked me if I was going out for the lead in the school Christmas play.

"They're doing A Christmas Carol," he informed me. "I'm thinking about trying out for Scrooge, but if you're going to try out I might not bother."

I thought it over a minute. The idea appealed to me.

"Scrooge, eh?" I replied thoughtfully. "Yeah, I might give it a shot."

Tyrone looked disappointed.

As I got up from the table, I gave him a pat on the back. "Don't feel bad, Ty," I said sympathetically. "You can probably still try out for one of the little unimportant parts."

The more I thought about the idea, the better I liked it. Who would be better in the school play than me? Who had more experience? Who had more guts? The lead in the Christmas play! The perfect thing to keep me in the public eye!

I could see it all now . . .

ALEXANDER B. FRANKOVITCH

starring as

SCROOGE

in

A *Christmas Carol*

I could make some posters with me posing in my Scrooge costume and sell them to small, unsuspecting children. Little kids too young to know what they're doing. Then I could use the poster money to hire an agent to get me jobs in Hollywood. Wow! Posters in Hollywood sell like hotcakes. Maybe I could have one with me all sweaty carrying a machine gun. Or one in the jungle where I'm . . .

"Alex . . . Alex . . . Alex!"

Raymond Vellenburg shouted me out of my daydream. When I looked up, he was halfway out the cafeteria door.

"The bell rang, Frankovitch! Where were *you*?"

As I picked up my books I couldn't help smiling.

"Hollywood," I muttered to myself. "I was in Hollywood."

☆

77

Tryouts were held on Thursday and Friday in the auditorium. The speech teacher, Mr. Tilton, was the director. He was tall and thin and had a skinny mustache that looked like he drew it on with a pencil. Also, he spoke with a British accent. I don't think he was British though. I think he just wanted to be.

On Wednesday afternoon he held a meeting to explain things. When I got to the auditorium, Mr. Tilton was already on stage clearing his throat.

"People, may I have your attention please? Tryouts will proceed thusly."

That's how he talked. He said stuff like "thusly."

"First of all I will give everyone a script, along with a sheet of paper describing the characters. There are a total of twenty-one parts available in this play. However, during tryouts all boys will read the part of Scrooge on page twenty-eight through thirty . . . and all girls will read the part of Mrs. Cratchit on pages fifty-five and fifty-six. This will make things immensely easier for yours truly.

"Questions thus far?"

Some kid in the front row raised his hand. "Who's yours truly?"

Mr. Tilton glared at the kid for about ten minutes. When you're trying to be British, you don't like a lot of kids making fun of you.

Finally some kid from the back of the room shouted out the answer. "Yours truly is *him*, stupid."

Mr. Tilton took a couple of deep breaths. I think he was trying to compose himself. If you ask me, guys like Mr. Tilton aren't cut out to be teachers. Guys like Mr. Tilton should play the violin.

"Any *other* questions?" he asked then.

Another hand went up. "What if you don't want to be in this play at all? Like what if your mom's just making you? Could you like not give us a part even if we're really talented?"

Before he could respond, a girl in front of me stood up and put her hands on her hips. "Why aren't there more girls' parts in this stupid play?" she demanded.

A couple of the boys in the back started booing. Pretty soon we were all doing it.

I stood up on my chair and cupped my hands.

"Where do I get my Scrooge costume?" I yelled. "Do I go to a tailor or what?"

It was a simple question, I thought. No need for Mr. Tilton to get upset like he did.

His cheeks puffed up like a balloon. Angrily, he stomped off the stage and began handing out scripts. "For those of you who are *truly* interested in being a part of this production, be here tomorrow at precisely three o'clock!" he snapped. "The decision as to who gets which role will be mine and mine alone. It will be based on how well you read your part."

He tried to calm himself down. "Those who seem most natural and at ease on the stage will have the best chance," he offered. "The best advice I can give you is to become familiar with the part. Then relax and just let it flow. Flow is very important."

This girl next to me took out a piece of paper and wrote down the word *flow*. I'm serious. She even put an exclamation point next to it. When she saw me looking, she covered her paper like it was a test or something.

I smiled smugly. "Don't worry. I'm a professional. I already know how to flow."

"Goody goody for you," she retorted.

My smile got even bigger.

Yeah. *Goody goody for me*, I thought happily. *Goody goody for old Alex "The Greatest Scrooge of All Time" Frankovitch.*

I had the best audition of anybody. I'm not kidding. I flowed like you wouldn't believe. I even added a line or two to make Scrooge seem more natural.

You should have seen me. It was the scene where Scrooge first sees the ghost of his old partner, Jacob Marley, and Jacob tells him about the spirits that are going to come and haunt him during the night.

Then Scrooge is supposed to say, "I choose not to see them, Jacob."

What a stupid thing to say! No one would be that calm! We're talking about ghosts here!

That's why my audition was so much better than anyone else's. When Jacob Marley told me about the spirits, I made Scrooge let out this giant, bloodcurdling scream.

"Ghosts! Oh no! Not ghosts!" I shrieked. "Come on, Jake! I hate stuff like that!"

It was great. More convincing than anything. That's why I could hardly believe my ears when Mr. Tilton stood on stage on Friday and announced the parts:

"People, may I have your attention please?" he began. "You all did an absolutely marvelous job, and I take great pleasure in announcing the cast of this year's Christmas play: Ebenezer Scrooge will be played by . . ."

I stood up.

"Albert Ruppert."

My knees caved in and I fell over.

Albert Ruppert? Was this a joke? That big show-off from my English class was actually going to be Scrooge? The kid who stands on his chair like a palace guard and announces the arrival of Mrs. Ballentine each day?

On stage Mr. Tilton was proceeding. "Skylar Fox will be Bob Cratchit; Cynthia Huggins will portray the Ghost of Christmas Past; Alexander Frankovitch will play Tiny Tim; Tyrone Hayes will be . . ."

Tiny Tim! Oh God, no! Not Tiny Tim! I *hate* Tiny Tim. I've *always* hated him! Ever since the first time I saw *A Christmas Carol* on television. Talk about unnatural. There he was, all pale and sick and skinny, walking around on that little crutch of his, and instead of whining and complaining like any normal kid would do, Tiny Tim spent his days smiling and "God blessing" people. He made me want to spit up.

Besides, he had no lines! A couple of quick prayers and a "thank you sir." What kind of acting do you call that?

I just couldn't figure it out. Albert Ruppert's audition had been the dumbest thing you ever saw! He was so nervous and twitchy, it made you squirmy just watching him.

Also, when he read his lines, he tried to make his voice real deep so he'd sound more grown-up. It's the way you make your voice sound when you're crank-calling someone and you want to sound like a man. It never works though. No matter how old you think you sound, as soon as you say, "Hello, is your toilet running?" people slam the phone down right in your ear.

After Mr. Tilton made the announcements, a lot of the cast started clapping for themselves and going crazy. It was like they had just won an Academy Award instead of a dumb part in a stupid school Christmas play. Albert Ruppert ran up on stage and started bowing. He wasn't doing it to be funny either. That's just how he acts. He's always telling you how great he is.

Annabelle Posey was the most obnoxious of all.

Even though she hadn't showed up for tryouts until Friday, she *still* got the part of Mrs. Cratchit. I don't know how she did it, but she did. You should have seen her. She started strutting around the stage like she was Jane Fonda or somebody.

Meanwhile, I just sat there with my knees caved in, shaking my head in disbelief. I felt angry and disappointed all at the same time. I had been so sure, so sure I'd get the part, I even memorized most of Scrooge's lines!

What had gone wrong? Hadn't Mr. Tilton seen me flow? Hadn't he noticed how natural I made Scrooge seem? Geez! If he'd wanted me to use my crank-call voice, he should have said so.

The more I thought about it, the sicker I got. After all, people were *counting* on me. Take the kids at the lunch table, for instance. They'd just started believing I was somebody special.

I covered my face with my hands. It wasn't fair. I'd probably be eating my lunch sideways for the rest of my life.

After a few minutes Annabelle Posey spotted me sitting alone in the back of the auditorium. She couldn't get there fast enough. Before I knew it, she was hovering over my seat, waiting for me to look up so she could laugh in my face.

I didn't do it though. I just kept my head bowed

and pretended not to notice her. That didn't stop old Annabelle, of course. She laughed right at the top of my head.

"Ha ha, Alex," she taunted. "I bet you thought you were going to get the lead, but you didn't. Too bad. What a shame. Guess you're just too skinny to be anyone but Teeny Tim."

That's how stupid she was. She called Tiny "Teeny."

I let her get away with it too. For the first time in my life, I didn't even feel like defending myself. Not even to Annabelle Posey.

Just then Mr. Tilton started speaking from the stage.

"Your attention again, please. . . .

"First I must thank everyone who tried out for the play. You were all wonderful, and the choices were very difficult to make. If you didn't get the part you wanted, I apologize. It doesn't mean you weren't good enough. It simply means there weren't enough good parts to go around.

"Also, if you didn't get a part and would like to work on scenery, on makeup, or on lighting, please see me and I'll sign you up. Believe me, working behind the scenes can be just as exciting as being on stage.

"The rest of the cast is dismissed. I'll see all of you

right here at three o'clock on Monday afternoon."

The room continued to buzz with excitement as cast members congratulated themselves all the way out the door. A few kids who hadn't gotten parts stayed and signed up for other committees. I guess I should have felt grateful that I'd gotten any part at all, but I didn't. Mostly I just felt pale and weak and sick.

Also I felt tired. Not sleepy tired though. More like my brain was tired or something. Tired of trying to believe in myself. Tired of letting myself down.

Finally I stood up, lowered my head in despair, and began shuffling slowly down the aisle. I felt like I weighed a million pounds. I know this sounds dramatic, but that's how I felt.

Mr. Tilton heard me shuffling. He looked up and waved.

"Ah, our Tiny Tim. You're going to be wonderful. I knew it as soon as I saw you on stage. A perfect Tiny Tim!"

I winced. That was me. That was who I was now. Tiny Tim Frankovitch. Weak, pale, skinny Tiny Tim Frankovitch.

I looked up and gave Mr. Tilton the feeblest of smiles.

"Godblessyousir," I mumbled pathetically. Then I plodded through the door.

☆

My parents wouldn't let me quit the play. I begged all weekend, but they wouldn't even listen.

At first my father tried to shame me into it. He took me firmly by the shoulders, looked me in the eye, and said, "You're no quitter, are you, son?"

I nodded eagerly. "Yes, I am, Dad. I'm a quitter. Accept it."

He let go of my shoulders. "You finish what you start, Alex," he said sternly. "It's as simple as that."

My mother nodded in agreement. "You're going to see the job through to the end, Alex."

Geez, they were making me sound like a carpenter! This wasn't a real job. Why couldn't some other little weak, pale, skinny kid see it through to the end?

☆

By Monday afternoon at three o'clock I'd hardly settled down at all. I showed up at rehearsal, but only because I had to. I guess you could say I had an attitude problem. And believe me, watching Albert and Annabelle strut around like superstars didn't help it one bit. In English class Albert told Mrs. Ballentine she could call him Ebenezer.

Mr. Tilton spent the first half-hour getting everyone organized. He handed out rehearsal schedules and explained them very carefully.

87

"People, do you all understand how this is going to work?" he called from the stage. "While one group is practicing scenes on stage, other groups will be going over their lines in different areas of the auditorium. Each day we will alternate so everyone gets plenty of stage time."

From two rows back I heard Annabelle giggle with anticipation. I turned around and stuck my finger down my throat like she was making me sick. What made me even sicker was that she and I were in all the same scenes.

Mr. Tilton walked around the auditorium and got each group started. Ours was first.

"Let's begin rehearsing the scene where the entire Cratchit family sits down to Christmas dinner," he suggested. "This is a very tender scene where Tiny Tim says grace. Work on it a while, and I'll be back to see how it's going."

I waited until I was sure he was gone. Then I opened my script, gritted my teeth, and solemnly began to read.

"Thank you, Lord, for giving us this fine goose for our Christmas feast. Please bless us all—even Mr. Scrooge."

"Why, thank you, Tiny Tim," said Annabelle as Mrs. Cratchit. "That was quite a lovely thought."

I looked up. That's when it hit me. An idea so

great I wondered why I hadn't thought of it before.

I smiled. "You're welcome, Mumsy," I said simply.

Annabelle jumped up out of her seat and whapped me in the head with her script. "It doesn't say that!" she growled. "I'm not Mumsy. Tiny Tim never called his mother Mumsy."

"I'm ad-libbing, Mumsy," I explained calmly. "Please pass the goose."

"Mr. Tilton!" screamed Annabelle. "Tell Alex that we're not allowed to ad-lib! Tell him to just read his lines like they're written!"

Mr. Tilton was busy with the people on stage. He waved his arms and told Annabelle to quiet down.

I just grinned. This was working out better than I could have imagined.

After that, I started ad-libbing more and more each day. Never in front of Mr. Tilton, of course. Only in our little groups. But it was especially fun to do it when Albert Ruppert was practicing with us. The kid was really beginning to get on my nerves. He acted like he was running the whole show.

"Okay, gang. Listen up," he said one day as he sat down to read lines with us. "In this scene I'm knocking on the door with my arms full of presents. Turn to page eighty, and let's take it from the top."

I rolled my eyes. Take it from the top. That's the

kind of stuff he'd say. Like he was conducting an orchestra or something.

"Knock, knock, knock," said Albert.

Skylar Fox, who played Bob Cratchit, pretended to open the door. "Please do come in, Mr. Scrooge. What a surprise this is!"

"Surprise, yes, I'm full of surprises," said Albert, pretending to set the packages down on the seat as he looked around. "Why, look here, Cratchit! These must be your fine children!"

"Yes, sir, they are. Let me introduce you, Mr. Scrooge. This is Tiny Tim, my youngest."

Albert held out his hand to shake. "And how are you this glorious Christmas Day, my boy?"

I took out a Kleenex and honked into it. Then I wadded it up and put it in his hand. "Could you throw this away please?"

Albert blew up. "Tiny Tim doesn't say that!" he yelled.

I shrugged my shoulders. "What's he supposed to do? Throw it on the floor?"

"Knock it off, Frankovitch," growled Albert. "If you don't knock it off, you're going to mess up the whole play.

"Now let's take it from the top again," he ordered, "and this time get it right.

"Knock, knock, knock."

"Please do come in, Mr. Scrooge," repeated Skylar, trying not to laugh. "What a surprise this is!"

"Surprise, yes, I'm full of surprises," said Albert, again. "Why, look here, Cratchit! These must be your fine children!"

"Yes, sir, they are. Let me introduce you, Mr. Scrooge. This is Tiny Tim, my youngest."

Cautiously, Albert held out his hand again. "And how are you this glorious Christmas Day, my boy?"

This time I shook his hand. "How do I look? Do I look healthy to you? Does this look like a healthy little body?"

Albert's face got red, but he decided to ignore me.

He turned to Annabelle. "And you, gentle lady, you must be Mrs. Cratchit?" he continued.

Annabelle curtsied. "Pleased to meet you, sir. Bob has told us a great deal about you."

I tapped Albert on the arm. "Her father's a clown, you know," I informed him pleasantly.

Skylar Fox started laughing. The rest of the kids sitting there did too. Everyone but Albert and Annabelle, that is. Albert and Annabelle practically exploded right out of their chairs. Then the two of them ran to the stage to tell Mr. Tilton.

You could hear Albert's voice echoing all over the school. "He's going to mess it up! I know he is! He's just waiting to mess it up!"

I sat back and grinned.

91

☆ *9* ☆

My mother invited the entire world to the play. She bought fifteen tickets and gave them away to anyone she could think of. She even gave one to my cousin Leon. The one with the grubby paws.

I guess I should have cared—all those people seeing me in such a humiliating part—but I didn't. I think I was past caring. And besides, I had Albert and Annabelle so nervous, it was almost worth the humiliation.

On the night of the play I hadn't even put my stuff down before Annabelle started making her stupid threats.

"I'm warning you, Alex," she blurted, standing there in her dumb Mrs. Cratchit outfit. "If you ruin this play, my father will see to it that you never work in show business again."

I looked her over. "Nice costume, Annabelle. The city dump will surprise you sometimes."

She stomped her foot.

"I *mean* it, Alex! I'm not kidding!"

I winked. "Neither am I, Mumsy."

Annabelle stormed away in such a frenzy, she didn't even notice Albert Ruppert coming through the door.

He was being so quiet, I almost missed him myself.

His Scrooge costume was in his hand. But instead of putting it on, he sat down in the closest chair and doubled over like he had just been punched in the stomach.

The expression on his face looked familiar. It's the same one you get when you're eating over at a friend's house and the kid's mother makes you try a new vegetable. It's usually brownish green, and it tastes so gross you can't swallow it; and you can't talk, and you can't spit it out. So you just sit there with this horrible expression until you figure out what to do with it. Usually I pretend to cough and spit it in my napkin. If I don't have a napkin, I put it in my pocket.

Anyway, the night of the play I watched Albert for several minutes before it finally dawned on me what was wrong. . . .

Albert Ruppert had stage fright! The more I

watched his face, the more positive I became. Old Albert Ruppert wasn't as sure of himself as he pretended to be.

A big grin began to spread across my face. *Hmmm,* I said silently. *Should I, or shouldn't I? Does Albert deserve a little teasing, or doesn't he?*

I thought back to that day in English class, the day after my commercial, when Albert had stood up and pretended to play the violin while everyone laughed. My grin got bigger. I had my answer.

Slowly, I sauntered over to where he was sitting and smiled down at him. Casually, I stood there cracking my knuckles.

"How's it going, Ebenezer?" I asked, rocking back and forth on my heels. "Pretty exciting, huh? Being the big star of the Christmas play. All those lines to remember in front of all those people. I was just counting the audience a minute ago. Five million and seven. I hope that doesn't make you nervous."

Albert was purple.

"I hope you don't forget your lines or anything, Al," I went on unmercifully. "In second grade, Bubby Greene forgot his lines and everyone started laughing their heads off. Bubby wet his pants. I hope something like that doesn't happen to you, Albert."

Albert's eyes opened real wide. It was a new worry he hadn't thought of before.

"Oh, by the way, Al. I've come up with a few little surprises for you during the play. You know, just to keep you on your toes. I think you'll really get a kick out of them."

That did it. Albert shot from his seat like a bullet. The next thing I knew he was heading down the hall toward the boys' bathroom.

It sort of surprised me, if you want to know the truth. I didn't know he'd react like that. I was just messing around, that's all. Where was his sense of humor?

Mr. Tilton saw him leave and rushed after him. Meanwhile, the clock on the wall kept ticking away. Six thirty . . . six forty-five . . . six fifty. Most of the cast members already had on their costumes and makeup. The play was scheduled to start at seven thirty.

I couldn't put it off any longer. I went into one of the little dressing rooms and came out with my sissy suit on. Little brown shorts, knee socks, a white shirt with a wide circular collar, and a big fluffy black bow tied at the neck. The bow was the worst. Tiny probably picked it out himself. He probably thought it looked sharp.

After I was dressed, I walked into the hall. The

boys' bathroom was down at the end, around the corner. I checked my watch. Five minutes after seven, and still no Albert.

I opened the auditorium door a crack and snuck a peek at the audience. It was packed. The whole city was in the auditorium, and Scrooge was in the boys' lavatory afraid he was going to wet his trousers.

Suddenly there was some commotion in the hallway behind me. I spun around just in time to see Mr. Tilton come screeching around the corner. He was charging in my direction with this crazy wild expression on his face. His hair was sticking out in all directions.

He was alone, too. Albert Ruppert wasn't anywhere to be seen.

Mr. Tilton was really cruising now. He hurdled a mop and bucket and never even broke stride.

"Quick! Quick! Quick!" he shouted at me as he screeched to a halt. "Do you know Scrooge? Do you? Do you know Scrooge?"

I took a few steps backward.

"Uh . . . do I know Scrooge?" I began cautiously. "Er, ah . . . yes. I know Scrooge, Mr. Tilton. Scrooge is Albert. Albert Ruppert. You know him too. Remember? Kind of a tall kid with—"

Mr. Tilton jumped up and down. He seemed to be having some sort of breakdown.

"No, no, no!" he yelled. "I mean, do you know Scrooge's *lines*! His part! He said you might. Do you?"

He was grabbing at my wide circular collar.

"I'm not sure," I sputtered. "I mean, when I was trying out for the part, I knew most of his lines. I guess I still do. I've heard them enough. Why? Is Albert sick or—"

"Down to the bathroom!" he interrupted. "Quick! Change clothes with Albert and get back here in ten minutes! I'll try to stall the audience!"

I stood there in a daze. "Geez, I don't know, Mr. T. I'm not sure I'm even in the mood for this anymore. I was at first, but—"

Mr. Tilton wasn't even listening. He gave me a push.

"Go! Hurry!" he called. "We're all counting on you! Albert won't do it, and we're counting on you!"

Another nudge. "Faster! Faster!" he urged.

Inside my head a million thoughts were swimming around at once. Was this really happening? Was I really headed down to the lavatory as Tiny Tim and coming back as Scrooge, the star of the play? I thought stuff like this only happened in . . .

The movies! Of course! That's what this was! Finally I was getting a scene right out of the movies. Something bad happens, and then something good happens to make up for it. This was my something good! I deserved it too. After all I'd been through, nobody deserved it more than me.

Okay, now think, Alex! Think! I ordered. *Can you handle this? Do you really know the lines like you said you did?*

"Bah! Humbug!" I bellowed confidently. "Bah! Humbug!"

By the time I reached the bathroom, my heart was pounding like crazy.

I took a deep breath. Now for Albert. Was he going to be nice about this? Or would he be crouching in the corner with some sort of weapon?

Cautiously I leaned inside. "Albert, I need your costume," I called softly.

There. That had been easy enough. Now I'd simply walk in and get it. If he had a machine gun, I'd call Mr. Tilton.

I swung the door open wide. Albert was standing over the sink by the window. The water was running and his face was wet.

He looked up. Only for a second. But I could tell he'd been crying.

He turned away to hide his face. Then, without saying a word, he took off Scrooge's coat and laid it on the sink next to the hat. After that he went into one of the little stalls, locked the door, and quietly began taking off the rest of the costume.

I didn't know what to say or do. When you're prepared for hand-to-hand combat, crying sort of catches you off guard.

Slowly I walked to the mirror and untied my fluffy bow. Albert tossed over his shirt.

"Thanks," I murmured awkwardly.

The rest of Scrooge's outfit followed. As it tumbled to the floor, Albert blew his nose.

I put the costume on as quickly as I could. The coat, the hat, the shirt, the pants—all of it. Too big, of course. But with the sleeves folded under and the pants legs pinned up, it wouldn't be bad.

I laid my Tiny Tim costume on the floor, where Albert could reach it. Then I covered my ears tightly so I couldn't hear the sniffling.

"I'm going now," I stated matter-of-factly.

I uncovered my ears in case he wanted to wish me good luck or something.

He didn't.

"Okay, then. Here I go. I'm going."

I paused again to listen. The sniffling had stopped. Now there was no sound at all.

Wait a minute. No sound at all?

"Albert?" I said, pounding on the locked door. "You're okay in there, aren't you?"

Nothing.

"Okay, Albert. Now listen very closely. You know that little story about Bubby Greene? Well, it

99

wasn't as bad as I made it sound. He hardly wet at all. He didn't even leave a puddle."

I knocked again.

"Albert?" I called. "Al?"

I was just about to peek under the door when he finally answered.

"Just get out of here, Alex! Just go!"

"Whew!" I said, relieved. "Albert, I thought you might be—"

"I'm sick," he blurted. "That's all. I'm just sick."

"Yeah. Sure you are, Albert," I agreed weakly.

For the next few seconds I stood there in silence and stared at the locked door in front of me. A lot of thoughts were racing through my mind. Racing so fast I couldn't sort them out.

I looked at my Scrooge reflection in the mirror. If this was my "something good," why was I so confused?

"This is great, Albert," I grumbled quietly. "You're taking all the fun right out of this for me."

"Just go," he ordered again.

This time I was the one who was silent.

"Alex, I said *go*."

Still nothing.

"Geez, Alex!" he shouted suddenly. "Why can't you just get out of here and leave me alone?"

"Because. That's why," I mumbled.

100

"That's no reason! Because *why*?" he demanded.

"Because . . . I don't know why!" I started to shout. "Because maybe I know how you feel, that's all!"

I took off Scrooge's jacket and threw it back over the door.

"There! Okay?"

Albert threw it back.

"Geez, Albert!" I shouted again. "Why are you making this so hard for me? I'm not going to mess it up, okay? Just do the stupid play! You're a good Scrooge, Albert! Don't you know that?"

I took off the rest of the costume and shoved it under the door.

Frantically I put on my Tiny Tim outfit and left.

☆

The play started fifteen minutes late.

It went well.

Albert Ruppert was the star.

☆ *10* ☆

I was just about to leave the auditorium when I heard him call.

"Alexander! Wait!"

Mr. Tilton came hurrying up behind me. His face looked real intense. Like there was something important on his mind.

As soon as I turned around, he began shaking my hand.

"Thank you, Alexander," he said solemnly.

"You're welcome, Mr. Tilton," I replied, trying not to look confused.

He put his hands on my shoulders and stared at me a second. Then he gave me a hardy bear hug—like we were two Alaskan fur traders who hadn't seen each other for a long time. What the heck was going on here?

102

"That was a wonderful thing you did for Albert tonight," he said at last.

Oh. So *that* was it.

"You could have starred in that play yourself, Alexander," he continued earnestly. "You know it. And I know it."

I nodded in agreement. "I know it."

"You didn't, though, did you?"

I shook my head no.

"And do you know why you didn't, Alexander?"

This one was trickier. To be honest, I still wasn't completely sure.

"Because you're an unsung quiet hero, that's why."

Quickly I gave another nod. "Right."

"I don't know how you did it. But somehow you were able to get Albert to play the part himself," he went on. "And in my book that makes you one of a handful of sensitive souls who go behind the scenes and quietly save the day."

I smiled. All of a sudden I felt a little bit like the Lone Ranger.

Mr. Tilton smiled too. "My hat's off to you, Alexander," he said. Then he bowed. "The quiet hero. The very best kind."

"Er, thanks. My hat's off to you, too, Mr. T."

☆

I've never been a hero before. Especially not a quiet one. Up until now I've never been a quiet anything.

I can tell you one thing though. Being a quiet hero is a lot harder than it sounds. I mean, it's bad enough that you have to go behind the scenes and quietly save the day. But the worse part comes when you have to stand around and grit your teeth while someone else gets all the glory. I'm serious. The Lone Ranger is probably down to his gums by now.

I didn't mind giving Albert the glory the night of the play so much. I probably wouldn't have remembered all the lines anyway. And besides, part of me was sort of proud of myself.

But by the next week, Albert Ruppert had really started getting on my nerves. He just wouldn't let it die, you know? He kept strutting around the cafeteria and squeezing me out of my place at the lunch table again. On Monday and Tuesday I sat with my tray sideways while he plopped himself down wherever he wanted.

"Hey, Ruppert! Over here!" someone would yell as soon as Albert walked into the lunchroom. "Hey, Scrooge, we've got a place for you!"

Then everybody would slide down and I'd get shoved into the wall.

"Move over, Frankovitch! Move down!"

After that, I had to listen as kids congratulated him and asked him ridiculous questions like was he going to be an actor when he grew up, and would he still remember them when he got to be a movie star?

But even that wasn't the worst part. The worst part was the smug look on his face. Like he was King Albert. King of the whole school.

I gritted my teeth about a thousand times. *A quiet hero, a quiet hero,* I'd think to myself. Sometimes I'd start humming the Lone Ranger theme song.

☆

Thursday was the day I finally cracked.

The lunch table was almost filled when I got there. It took me forever to squeeze in and make a little place for myself. I had just started to open my milk when I saw Albert standing at the end of the table with his tray.

"Hey, Frankovitch! Move, so Al can sit down!" called Raymond Vellenburg. "You just took his seat."

I just kept opening my milk.

"*Now,* Alex," ordered Chad Jones. "Move it. We promised Albert we'd save him a seat, and you just took it."

Out of the corner of my eye I saw King Albert start down the aisle with his tray. He stopped right behind me. Then he stood there waiting. Waiting like a vulture for my seat. I couldn't believe it! Hadn't I done enough for the jerk? Hadn't I let him be Scrooge? Did I owe him my seat, too?

Something inside me snapped. I jumped up and threw my tray on the table behind me.

"Oh, I'm sorry, Albert! Here! Sit! I forgot! You're the star. You deserve it!"

Albert didn't even look at me. He just turned his head and put his tray on the table where mine had been. Geez! He was going to do it! He was actually going to take my seat!

"Hey, I've got an idea, Al!" I went on. "As long as you're sitting there, why don't you tell these guys some more about the play?

"Why don't you tell them why it was fifteen minutes late? That's a funny story, don't you think?"

I slapped him on the back. "Don't you, Albert old buddy?"

Slowly, he turned around on the bench and looked up at me. His shoulders slumped over in defeat. I had him, and he knew it.

I gave him a nasty little grin. "What'd you say, Al? Do you want to tell them, or should I?"

He never stopped looking at me. Never even

blinked. He just sat there staring until finally he spoke.

"What took you so long, Alex?" he whispered.

The words stung. Worse than if he'd hit me. I can't explain it any other way.

I sat back down.

I didn't tell.

☆

I don't see Albert much these days. Once in a while at noon, but that's about it. We look at each other sometimes. Then we look away.

Right now I'm just sort of letting my life get back to normal. I'm not going to end up on a cereal box. Not this time anyway.

Brian and I are best friends again. Annabelle Posey and I are still worst enemies. I accidentally drew a mustache on her art project, and she reported me to the office.

Ned the Bully is still Ned the Bully. Last week he told me my face smelled. Then he took me by the shoulders and jumped me up and down a few times. I felt a little silly, but nothing was broken.

☆

I ended my fan club right after the play. Ernest and Fluffy had started goofing off in the meetings.

Besides, Ernest insisted on bringing his potty seat, and there was just something degrading about it.

I'd like to start another club someday. I don't know what kind yet. Something I can be president of, though. I'm sure I'll want to be president.

I've stopped thinking about being a star. At least for now I have. I'm sort of in a rest period. In between dreams, you might say.

When you're in between dreams, you get to lean back and relax and stop trying so hard. Trying to be somebody, I mean. It's not as exciting as being a television star, but it's not that bad, either. You just have to learn to be satisfied with the way you are for a while. Not forever. Just until you're finished resting.

That's what I'm doing right now. I'm trying to be satisfied just being me.

Plain old me.

Plain old Alex.

Plain old Alex "The Greatest Quiet Hero of All Time" Frankovitch.

Barbara Park

is one of the most popular authors writing for young readers today. Her previous titles are *Skinnybones, The Kid in the Red Jacket, Buddies, Beanpole, Operation: Dump the Chump,* and *Don't Make Me Smile.*

Ms. Park holds a B.S. in education from the University of Alabama and lives in Phoenix, Arizona, with her husband and two sons.